Dear Parents and Teachers:

Realistic fiction is ideal for readers transitioning from picture books to chapter books. In Rourke's Beginning Chapter Books, young readers will meet characters that are just like them. They will be drawn in by the familiar settings of school and home and the familiar themes of sports, friendship, feelings, and family. Young readers will relate to the characters as they experience the ups and downs of growing up. At this level, making connections with characters is key to developing reading comprehension.

Rourke's Beginning Chapter Books offer simple narratives organized into short chapters with some illustrations to support transitional readers. The short, simple sentences help readers build the needed stamina to conquer longer chapter books.

Whether young readers are reading the books independently or you are reading with them, engaging with them after they have read the book is still important. We've included several activities at the end of each book to make this both fun and educational.

By exposing young readers to beginning chapter books, you are setting them up to succeed in reading!

Enjoy,
Rourke Educational Media

Table of Contents

Kickin' It

By Meg Greve
Illustrated by Alida Ruggeri

Rourke
Educational Media
rourkeeducationalmedia.com

www.rourkeeducationalmedia.com

Edited by: Keli Sipperley
Cover layout by: Renee Brady
Interior layout by: Rhea Magaro
Cover and Interior Illustrations by: Alida Ruggeri

Library of Congress PCN Data

Kickin' It / Meg Greve
(Rourke's Beginning Chapter Books)
ISBN (hard cover)(alk. paper) 978-1-63430-370-5
ISBN (soft cover) 978-1-63430-470-2
ISBN (e-Book) 978-1-63430-566-2
Library of Congress Control Number: 2015933727

Printed in the United States of America,
North Mankato, Minnesota

1
Goals and Dreams

The sun beat down on his head. Sweat stung his eyes. The crowd roared so loud he couldn't hear himself think. The only thing between him and true glory was a giant octopus standing in front of the goal. The octopus's tentacles were waving everywhere. Where could he shoot? Finally, Luis focused on the ball and kicked with all his might.

The crowd roared!

Then all he heard was Boo! and laughter. He squinted at the goal. The octopus had caught his ball with one quick swipe. NO! The Mighty Sharks lost the championships.

Luis sat straight up in bed. His hair was sticking up and his sheets were twisted all around him. Thank goodness! It was just a bad dream. He jumped up and grabbed his soccer jersey. Today was his first day of soccer camp. He couldn't wait to get out there and show off his amazing soccer skills.

2
It's Not as Easy as You Think

Luis always wanted to play on a soccer team. His parents finally signed him up this year. They were always too busy at work to remember in time. But his mom put it on her calendar and his dad did too, just to be sure. Now he was on a team called the Mighty Sharks. To Luis, the team name sounded like they would be winners. He was sure they would be with him on it.

Luis knew he would be great on the field. He watched soccer on TV and read as much as he could about the sport. He practiced kicking the ball in the backyard and daydreamed about it in school instead of doing his math.

During recess, he played with the other kids in pick-up games. He always made sure he had the ball and scored as many goals as he could, without passing to anyone else. Sometimes the other kids got mad at him for that. He didn't think about it too much though because his team always won anyway. They are just mad they aren't the ones who scored all those goals, Luis thought.

As he and his mom pulled up to the field, Luis's heart thumped. There were kids and soccer balls everywhere. He heard whistles, shouts, and the *Smack!* sound a ball makes when it is kicked.

Luis felt a rush of joy. Finally he was where he wanted to be.

They walked over to the registration desk. When Luis told him his name and age, the man behind the desk pointed him toward his team. He said goodbye to his mom and rushed over to meet his new teammates.

He ran up to a group of boys wearing the same jersey he had on.

"Hi, I'm Luis," he said to a boy with short, curly hair.

"What's up? I'm Matt and this is Roberto. What position do you play?"

"Striker," Luis said. "I score the most goals at my school."

Matt and Roberto looked at each other and rolled their eyes. They started passing the ball back and forth, ignoring Luis. Luis shrugged his shoulders and started talking to another boy holding a ball.

"Hi I'm Luis," he said.

"Hey, I'm Will." he replied. He started to kick a ball back and forth with his feet. Luis was amazed. Will never seemed to lose control of the ball. He kicked it high into the air and headed the ball in Luis's direction. Luis was so surprised that he didn't have time to move. The ball slammed into his nose, which started gushing blood. Luis was shocked. He didn't know what to do and just stood there while Will went to get the coach.

The coach came running over. "What happened?" he asked.

"I kicked the ball to him and he missed it," Will said with a grin. "Sorry dude, I didn't know you couldn't see." Some of the boys snickered as the coach held a towel to Luis's nose. Luis was miserable. His first time on the field with his new team and he missed his chance to show them how great he is.

"Leave him alone," said another boy next to Luis. "We all miss a ball once in awhile. Give him a break." He turned and looked at Luis. "My name is Ty. Welcome to the Mighty Sharks!"

Luis smiled through the towel and mumbled, "Nice to meet you." He sounded like he was underwater. He really wanted to crawl under a rock.

"Okay, Sharks, hit the field. Luis, you wait until you can get that bleeding under control," the coach said. The team ran out on the field and took a lap.

Luis watched practice for awhile. The team looked really good. Luis had never seen anything like it. They were doing moves he had never seen before. Still, he felt that he was sure to be one of the best once he got his chance.

Finally, his nose stopped bleeding and he ran out to join the team. This was it. This was his chance! Just then, he felt a tug on his shoe, tripped, and fell over. This time even the coach laughed a little. Luis got up, tied his shoe, and rubbed his sore elbow while running to join the team in drills.

For the rest of the practice, Luis tried to stay out of everyone's way. Any chance he got with the ball, he immediately tried to shoot it into the goal even when he knew he wouldn't get it in. The coach yelled at him a couple of times, and his teammates made some comments, but he just ignored it all. He did what he was sure he should do. His new friend Ty looked at him strangely a couple of times, but Luis just kept going.

At the end of practice, their coach gave a speech about working together and playing like a team. He never said anything about making sure they won a game. He congratulated a couple of boys who did a good job passing to one another, but that seemed weird to Luis. Why pass the ball when you have it? The goal is to make a GOAL. He saw his mom waiting for him and started jogging to the car. Suddenly, he felt that familiar tug on his shoe. He had time to yell out before he hit the ground again.

Ty was right behind him and let out a little laugh. "You need to learn to tie your shoes and pass the ball, dude."

He shook his head and laughed a little more. "Do you even know how to tie your shoes?"

Luis was confused. Ty had been so friendly at practice. He was great about passing the ball to him. Why was he being so rude now?

His mom honked the horn. He hopped up without tying his shoes, and started toward the car again. He was careful not to step on his shoelaces. They kept swinging around both of his ankles. He felt a little silly, but he was in a hurry to get away from the boys on the field.

He slumped into the car and slammed the door.

"How was soccer?" his mom asked.

"Pretty bad." Luis said. "I fell twice, got a bloody nose, and didn't make a single goal. I am not sure I want to go back tomorrow."

"Sometimes trying something new and learning new skills can be frustrating and scary. Stick with it. You love playing it at school, and once you get the hang of playing on a real team, you will love it." His mom patted him on the head and pulled away into traffic.

3
Another Shot

Luis was running down the field, dribbling the ball. He looked at the octopus with no fear. This time, he would get past the waving tentacles. This time, he would be the hero and score the winning goal. The people in the stands were wild with excitement. But all he could hear was his breath and the little taps his feet made as he kicked the ball.

"Luis! Luis! Luis!" The crowd chanted his name.

Then, in slow motion, he kicked the ball with all his might—and missed!

He tripped over the ball. The octopus grabbed it with one long arm, and the ref blew the whistle. The familiar groans and boos of the crowds filled the air.

"LUIS!"

Luis sat straight up. His mom was shouting his name. It was just another bad dream. What a relief.

"Luis! Hurry up! You overslept, and now you are going to be late for soccer camp."

He jumped up, threw on his jersey and ran downstairs.

On the way to practice, he thought about the day before and all of the embarrassing mistakes he made. He was determined not to do the same thing again. He would show everyone how good he really is and make them proud that he is part of the team.

When his mom pulled up, everyone was already out on the field running the first drills. Luis looked down to check and make sure his laces were tied. They were. No tripping on them today! He jogged over to the team and said hi to everyone.

"Hi, Coach, I overslept this morning. I promise it won't happen again." Luis said.

"You bet it won't," Coach said. "Take a lap to help you remember to be here on time." Coach blew his whistle and set up for the next drill. Ty shrugged his shoulders at Luis and ran to get in line. Luis was frustrated, but started taking his lap. That's when he noticed he was missing one of his shin guards.

Oh no, Luis thought. *If Coach notices, he won't let me play. Maybe he won't be able to tell.*

As Luis finished his lap, he ran over to the team to join in the practice. The drill was set up so that the ball was rolled between two players. Both players tried to get the ball and dribble it past the other. Luis knew he would be excellent at this. He was matched up with Will. This made him a little bit nervous, but he was determined to prove himself. The ball was rolled between him and Will. Will kicked at the ball just as Luis got closer.

Will missed the ball and kicked Luis in the shin instead. The shin without the guard!

Luis fell down, grabbing his shin. The pain was horrible. The coach blew the whistle and knelt down next to Luis.

"Where is your shin guard, Luis?" he asked.

"I guess I forgot it," Luis mumbled. He was so embarrassed. Forgetting your equipment is such a beginner's mistake!

"Well, you should have told me. I always have extra. Now you have to sit out and ice your shin until you are better." Luis wished he had told Coach. Now he was hurt and sitting out of practice. Camp was getting worse and worse.

He watched while the team played a practice game. The boys passed back and forth to each other as they ran up and down the field. Luis was confused.

Not many of them tried to score a goal. They always seemed to be looking to get rid of the ball, instead of shooting it. When they did shoot the ball, the ball almost always went into the net for a goal. I am just as good as they are. I would have been shooting at the goal way more though, thought Luis. His shin felt better, so he asked the coach if he could borrow a shin guard and joined in practice.

Coach put him in the game. The boys were calling his name when he got the ball. Wow, he thought, they are all calling my name. They must think I am really good. He saw his chance to score a goal. One of the players from the other team got in his way, though. He could hear Ty calling his name and telling him he was open. He ignored him and tried to dribble around the other player. The boy got the ball away from Luis and started kicking the ball up the field.

"Luis! I was open! Why didn't you pass it to me?" Ty yelled. He looked really mad.

"I wanted to make the shot," Luis said. "You should have been blocking that guy to help me out."

"No, you should have passed it to me. That's how we play on this team." Ty said.

Luis wondered if he would ever feel like he was a part of the team. He was always making mistakes and making other people mad at him. The coach blew his whistle. Practice was finally over. Luis ran to his mom's car without saying goodbye to anyone.

"How was camp today?" asked his mom.

"Horrible," Luis said. "I forgot a shin guard and got kicked in the shin. I had to sit out and ice it for awhile while the other kids were playing a game. Then when I got to play, I made everyone mad at me. I don't know what to do."

His mom patted his arm.

"Don't give up, Luis. Remember how to play on a team. You are not the only one. There are other players, and you can only do well with the help of everyone," she said.

Luis looked out the window as they pulled away. He thought about what his mom said. Maybe she's right, he thought.

4
Getting the Glory

The sun was in his eyes. Sweat dripped down his back. He was running as fast as he could toward his teammate. The octopus was back, waving his arms around. The crowd was cheering and screaming. When the ball was passed to him, he pulled his leg back to kick as hard as he could toward the goal. Out of the corner of his eye, he noticed another player on his team. He was wide open with a clear shot. Luis stopped for a second, and then passed the ball to the other boy. The boy kicked the ball and scored the winning goal.

BEEP, BEEP, BEEP!

Luis set an alarm before bed the night before so he wouldn't oversleep. He hit the snooze button, but got up anyway. He was thinking about the dream he had. Why didn't I take the shot this time? It seems like such a waste to not try and score yourself. Then no one will notice how good you are. The other guy will get all of the glory.

When Luis got to the field that morning, he could tell that the guys weren't happy with him. He tried to smile and say hi to Ty, but Ty just turned his back and practiced dribbling his ball. The coach called everyone over to the bench.

"Okay guys, today is the day. We are going to have a game against the other camp team, the Purple Octopuses. They are really tough. We are going to practice for awhile before the game." As Coach called out who was going to start in the game, Luis kept waiting to hear his name. "Will, Ty, Andy, Jorge, Cole, and Charlie, you are the starters."

Luis's shoulders slumped. Why wasn't he starting? Now he would have to sit on the bench and wait. He was really confused. He felt like he did really well over the past two days. He did make a couple of mistakes, but nothing big. Luis decided to ask the coach.

"Coach, when do I get to play in the game?" Luis asked.

"Everyone gets a chance, but I had to choose the players who prove they know how to play on a team. You need to work on that," he said.

Luis lined up to practice with the team. He felt a little ashamed of himself. He started to realize how selfish he had been. No wonder the guys were being so unfriendly.

Luis walked over to Ty and said, "Congratulations on starting, Ty. You really deserve it."

"Thanks, Luis. I hope we beat these guys." Ty said. He gave Luis a fist bump as he ran out to the field.

5
The Real
Purple Octopus

The Mighty Sharks and the Purple Octopuses were evenly matched. The score was tied. Luis got to sub in a couple of times, but didn't really get to touch the ball. Finally, they were down to the last minutes of the game.

"Luis! You're in," the coach yelled.

Luis sat up on the bench. He couldn't believe that this was his chance. He ran out on the field, giving Andy a high-five on his way. Play started and Luis focused on the ball.

He got the ball and started running down the field toward the goal. The crowd was cheering. Sweat was streaming down his face. He knew this was his moment. He noticed that one of the Purple Octopuses was coming toward him. The goal was in his sight, but he wasn't sure he would be able to get a clear shot. From the corner of his eye, he saw Ty. Ty was wide open and close to the goal. Should he take the shot or pass?

Luis remembered the coach's words. He thought about how his mom said he needed to work with everyone. At the last minute, he yelled to Ty and passed the ball. Ty kicked it in for the goal.

The Mighty Sharks won!

6
A Team Player

BEEP, BEEP, BEEP! The alarm went off. Luis sat up. Weird, no soccer dream last night, he thought. He jumped out of bed, put on his jersey, grabbed his shoes and shin guards, and ran downstairs for breakfast.

"Great game yesterday, Luis," Ty said when he got to the field.

"Thanks, you took a great shot!" Luis said. He smiled at Ty. Finally he felt like he was part of the Mighty Sharks. He didn't realize how lonely it could feel when you don't play as part of the team.

Coach blew the whistle and called the team over. "Okay guys, we are playing the Barracudas today. Here are the starters, "Ty, Andy, Cole, Jorge, Charlie, and Luis."

"Hey, Luis," Ty yelled, "your shoes are untied!"

Luis grinned. He knew he was going to love being part of this team.

Reflection

Dear Reader,

I am so glad I got the chance to play with the Mighty Sharks. Learning to play on a team can be tough. Ty really helped me to take the chance and count on others. I know winning isn't everything, but it is really fun to share a win with others.

Your pal,
Luis

Discussion Questions

1. What lessons did Luis learn from his teammates?

2. Why do you think Luis didn't dream about the octopus on day four?

3. What do you think might have happened if Luis had not passed the ball to Ty during the game?

4. What advice do you think Luis would give to new players on the team?

5. Describe Ty using at least three character traits. Give examples from the story to support your descriptions.

Vocabulary

Look back in the story to find these words. How does the author use them? Can you define each word?

determined
equipment
focused
glory
miserable
nervous
registration
shin
snickered

Writing Prompt

Pretend you are a newspaper reporter writing an article about the Mighty Sharks. Describe the game they played against the Purple Octopuses. Be sure to include details about the important plays and players.

Q & A with Author Meg Greve

Did you play soccer?
I did play soccer throughout my childhood and into high school. I was never the star on the team. I often forgot my equipment, and never scored a goal. I still loved it though. Mostly because I played with all of my friends!

Do your children play soccer?
My son, Will, plays soccer. He loves to play, and I even helped coach his team last year. My daughter, Madison, plays basketball. Both kids really like playing on a team.

What is your favorite sport?
My favorite sport is actually tennis. It is not as much of a team sport, unless you play doubles.

Organize a Soccer Party!

Get a group of friends together to play soccer. Separate your friends into two teams. Create team names, make jerseys, and write a team cheer.

After the game, share a picnic at the field with all of your friends and their families. To make the day really fun, play some of these silly versions of soccer.

Websites to Visit

www.kids-play-soccer.com/basic-soccer-rules

www.all-youth-soccer-training.com/soccer-facts

www.active.com/baseball/articles/5-tips-to-be-a-good-team-player

About the Author

Meg Greve writes mostly nonfiction children's books. In order to write fiction, she had to remember when she was a kid and then change the story to make it more interesting. She played soccer, but never scored a goal, cut her own hair at a sleepover, and had fights with her best friend (but always made up)! Almost all of the story is from her imagination, but some of it has a little bit of truth. Can you guess which parts?

About the Illustrator

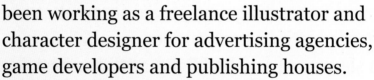

My name is Alida Ruggeri.
I was born in 1983 in
Milan (Italy) but currently
I'm based in London.
After a triennal course
at School of Comics in
Milan, since 2008 I've
been working as a freelance illustrator and
character designer for advertising agencies,
game developers and publishing houses.

In 2012 I won the 1st place "Pitch Me!
Awards" promoted by RAI (the National
Italian Broadcasting Company), with the
proposal of the animated cartoon series
"Fang You!"

I love drawing funny characters and
stupid things to put a smile on everybody's
face!"